Mountains

DISCOVER PICTURES AND FACTS ABOUT MOUNTAINS FOR KIDS! A CHILDREN'S TOPOGRAPHY BOOK

You've probably seen a few mountains all around, but you'll learn some helpful and cool facts about mountains that are all around you, and why they matter.

Mountains take millions of years to form, whether they're made from volcanoes that long died out, or when plates slam up against one another.

Mountains are millions of years old in many cases, and even the tallest mountains were formed long ago.

Mountains are not only pretty, but they actually provide shelter during stormy weather, and also water when there isn't any snow, and they also offer a sanctuary for plants and animals.

Sometimes a volcano doesn't' erupt through the crust, but there's lava underneath it, and they're called a dome mountain. The Black Hills of South Dakota is an example of this

The highest point of a mountain is the summit or peak

Plateau mountains are actually square-looking mountains that form when tectonic plates collide with one another but don't buckle the surface of this

There is actually no solid definition of a mountain because some scientists say it's one size, some say it's another size.

Mt. Fuji was actually one of the first mountains that were part of a story, and that story is called The Tale of the Bamboo Cutter, which is Japan's first recorded story

The largest mountain isn't actually on Earth, but it's actually on Mars, but it's actually got a large magma hotspot that triggers this

One of the easiest high-elevation mountains to climb is Mount Kilimanjaro in Africa, and it requires no gear or experience, but you do experience altitude sickness

Mountains are pretty, but they are vital to our world. Here you learned a little bit about mountains, and why they matter

Lightning Source UK Ltd.
Milton Keynes UK
UKHW050950141222
413907UK00006B/46